BUMBLEBEE

KU-351-656

ROBOT MODE: One of the most compact members of Team Prime

VEHICLE MODE: Muscle car

MARKINGS: Yellow and black armour

KEY WEAPON: Stingers

POWER MATCH: Soundwave – they are both scouts, but for opposing teams

STARSCREAM

ROBOT MODE: Smaller than Megatron, but deadly to any humans and most Autobots

VEHICLE MODE: Alien fighter jet

MARKINGS: Black armour with bright red markings

KEY WEAPON: Null Missiles

POWER MATCH: Bulkhead – this Bot and Con are complete opposites in every way

901618225X

TRA
Optimus

FORMERS
P R I M E

OPTIMUS UNDER
THREAT

DON'T MISS ANY
OF THE ADVENTURES:

MEGATRON RETURNS

TRANS FORMERS
PRIME

OPTIMUS UNDER THREAT

BANTAM BOOKS

TRANSFORMERS PRIME: OPTIMUS UNDER THREAT
A BANTAM BOOK 978 0 857 51111 9

First published in Great Britain by Bantam
A Random House Group Company

1 3 5 7 9 10 8 6 4 2

The Random House Group Limited supports the Forest Stewardship Council
(FSC®), the leading international forest certification organization. Our books
carrying the FSC label are printed on FSC®-certified paper. FSC is the only forest
certification scheme endorsed by the leading environmental organizations,
including Greenpeace. Our paper procurement policy can be found at
www.randomhouse.co.uk/environment.

Set in 15/20pt Bembo Regular

Bantam Books are published by Random House Children's Books,
61–63 Uxbridge Road, London W5 5SA

www.**kids**at**randomhouse**.co.uk
www.**totallyrandombooks**.co.uk
www.**randomhouse**.co.uk

Addresses for companies within The Random House Group Limited can be found
at: www.randomhouse.co.uk/offices.htm

THE RANDOM HOUSE GROUP Limited Reg. No. 954009

A CIP catalogue record for this book is available from the British Library.

Printed and bound by CPI Group (UK) Ltd, Croydon, CR0 4YY

THE AUTOBOTS

Optimus Prime
The Autobot leader will stop at nothing to protect Earth.

Bumblebee
Brave and very loyal, Bumblebee communicates with humans by bleeping.

Bulkhead
This Autobot is big, strong and really heavy. Bulkhead is kind of shy, too!

THE AUTOBOTS

Arcee
Arcee fights like a ninja and her vehicle mode is a super speedy motorbike.

Ratchet
The Autobot medic, Ratchet, is a techno genius.

THE DECEPTICONS

Megatron
The evil leader of
the Decepticons,
Megatron, wants to use
Dark Energon to
conquer Earth.

Starscream
Megatron's second-in-
command, Starscream, is
sneaky and evil.

Soundwave
A silent spy, Soundwave
can tap into and record
any kind of electronic
transmission.

Chapter One

ALL HAIL STARSCREAM

The Decepticon Spacebridge is in orbit over the Earth. The portal is open and a huge mass of Terrorcons swarm towards the threshold where their leader, Megatron, awaits them, eager to unleash his dark army on the Earth and achieve total domination . . . However, suddenly, without warning, there is an almighty explosion and in the next moment the entire Spacebridge is swallowed up by a vast blue and white fireball . . .

'Such a shame.' Starscream's voice dripped with sarcasm.

The evil Decepticon froze the image on

the screen that he was watching on board the spaceship *Nemesis*. Previously second-in-command, he had now appointed himself leader. 'But I applaud you, Megatron . . . you certainly made a grand exit.' He chuckled with satisfaction, his gaze lingering on the image of his former master's destruction.

Just then, he became aware of another Decepticon approaching him on the deck. 'Ah, Soundwave,' he said, quickly glancing over his shoulder, unable to fully take his eyes away from the screen. 'I wish to address the troops.'

Soundwave responded with the slightest nod – he obeyed his new master yet he did not seem to fully trust him.

'The loss of Megatron, leader of the Decepticon uprising, is certainly a blow to our cause.' A huge image of Starscream filled the audio-visual screens dotted around the spaceship. Decepticon troopers had stopped what they were doing and gathered to listen to Starscream's address. 'Yet we must not despair over his tragic demise but instead embrace the ultimate sacrifice he made, and build upon the foundation he laid with fresh ideas, a clearer vision and' – Starscream's voice had increased steadily in volume and, now, as he reached the climax of his speech, he made a fist and waved it in the air – 'an even mightier hand.'

'With all due respect, Commander Star . . . Er, Lord Starscream . . .' One of the troopers raised his hand and stepped towards the platform that Starscream was speaking from.

'Yes, yes, what is it?' Starscream snapped at him, obviously annoyed by the interruption.

The trooper continued regardless, 'If we failed to conquer Earth under Lord Megatron's command, what hope do we have now, while the Autobots still defend it?'

'Let me be clear.' Starscream's reply was steely. 'I studied for millennia under our former Master. Thus I am equipped to lead you. I, Megatron's true heir: Lord Starscream, Emperor of Destruction!' Starscream's voice had risen again to almost a scream, as he raised both hands and commanded the troops, 'HAIL ME!'

But his words had little impact on the gathered Decepticons, who stared back at him blankly, murmuring to one another, united in their discontent.

The audio-visual cut out as Starscream

marched away from the platform, furious at the troopers' response. Soundwave trailed obediently behind him, saying nothing.

'What use are troops who can't rise to the task of inflicting unspeakable destruction in my name?' Starscream grumbled bitterly to himself. Then he stopped beside one of the many display screens, deep in thought. 'I know of *one* capable warrior . . .' He suddenly brightened. 'One who exists here upon this very planet. One who can be student to MY master . . .' Finally, he turned to face Soundwave, issuing him with a direct order: 'And *you*, Soundwave, shall help me find him.'

Chapter Two

SCIENCE PROJECTS

Meanwhile down on Earth, in a secret location in the Nevada desert, Optimus Prime stood alone in a corner of the Autobots' headquarters, also deep in thought.

His comrade, Ratchet, a smaller Autobot, approached him.

'Optimus, why so glum? This planet – *all* planets – are finally free of Megatron's tyranny,' he said happily, his eyes shining.

Optimus continued to stare out into the middle distance, his blue eyes dimmer than usual. 'I do not disagree, Ratchet,' he replied flatly. 'It's just – a small part of me hoped to change Megatron's *mind*, not extinguish his spark.

'His vileness was not slain by your hand, Optimus,' Ratchet said sharply, 'but by his own twisted arrogance!' His temper flared, and then, seeing that his forcefulness wasn't snapping Optimus out of his gloom, he tried a softer approach. 'I'm sorry. I know the two of you had quite a history.'

'But the Megatron whom I once fought beside perished eons ago – the day he chose to become a Decepticon.' Prime shook his head. 'You're right: this is no time to brood,' he said, beginning to sound more like his usual self as he turned round to face his old friend. Although he was younger than Ratchet, the blue and red Prime Bot stood a good head taller and his plating was battle-worn and scratched. 'The Decepticons may be in disarray,' Optimus continued, 'but they aren't without leadership; and while Starscream is no Megatron, he is far from predictable—'

BOOM! A small explosion shook the base, causing Ratchet and Optimus a moment of unsteadiness before they leaped into action.

'*Decepticons!*' exclaimed Ratchet, glancing in the direction that the blast had come from, where sparks were flying. 'We're under attack!'

He and Optimus sprinted round the corner, and then stopped in their tracks in front of a small model volcano, which was pouring out smoke.

'It's no attack, Ratchet. It's my volcano,' Raf said between coughs, trying to clear the smoke by waving his arms.

'*Was* my volcano,' the boy added as the papier-mâché model collapsed in front of him.

'Hold still, Bulkhead – Jupiter needs its red spot.' Miko's voice came from another corner, and Ratchet swung round to see the big green Bot, Bulkhead, sitting on the floor holding a mobile of Earth's solar system, which the Japanese girl was dabbing at with a loaded paintbrush. There were pools of brightly coloured paint all over the metal floor.

'*What* in the AllSpark is going on

here?' demanded Ratchet.

'Our science projects are due tomorrow,' piped up Jack from where he was working. There was an open tool-box by his side and various engine parts were scattered around. The female Autobot, Arcee, appeared to be assisting her teenage friend in his attempt to assemble a motorbike engine.

'Maybe it needs one of these ... thingies?' she suggested brightly, picking up a bolt, evidently not fazed by Ratchet's grumpiness.

'You're a *motorcycle*, Arcee.' Jack chuckled. 'Shouldn't you know how to build a motorcycle *engine*?'

'You're a human, Jack. Can you build me a small intestine?' Arcee shot back at the teenager.

Ratchet shook his head, not believing what he was hearing.

'You can't work on these "projects" in here, you're' – he scrabbled around for an excuse – 'making a mess!'

Raf blinked up at the towering Autobot. 'But the Science Fair's a big part of our exam,' he informed him, pushing his glasses up his nose.

'Yeah,' Miko joined in. 'If Bulkhead doesn't help me finish this model of our solar system—'

'*Oh?*' replied Ratchet sarcastically. 'And what does Bulkhead know of *your* solar system? Or Bumblebee of your volcanoes, or—'

'Arcee of our motorcycles?' Jack finished for him.

'Precisely. We're not Earthlings . . .'

Ratchet said forcefully. 'And *they're* not scientists.' He gestured to his fellow Bots.

Optimus, who until now had been silently observing the whole exchange, finally spoke.

'But the Autobots *are* their guardians, Ratchet. Would it hurt to learn more of Earth, by helping our young friends with their schoolwork?' he suggested gently.

'Maybe our "young friends" should try learning more of *Cybertron*,' Ratchet grumbled – but having been put in his place by his leader, it was more of a complaint than an attack.

Chapter Three

A GREAT WARRIOR

'During the Great War, so much Energon was hidden on this forsaken rock . . .' Starscream said, sweeping his arm over the desert canyon that lay beneath the rocky cliff he stood on. They had left the *Nemesis* far away, up in space, and journeyed down to Earth in search of the mysterious 'student' Starscream had spoken of.

Soundwave stood behind his master, a rotating radar attached to his back that let out the occasional *ping*. The landscape around them was the same for as far as the eye could see – desert mountains and ravines all a parched sand-colour, with not a glimpse of any greenery or any other form of life.

'Our departed master sent some of Cybertron's greatest to guard it: *true warriors*, now lying in stasis, waiting to be reawakened.' Starscream's voice was full of pride at the thought of the powerful army that lay sleeping in the ground before him; an army that he could awaken and claim as his own. He paused for a minute, thinking it over, a small smile playing on his lips.

'Such folly that, late in life, Megatron searched distant space for warriors, rather than here beneath his feet.' Starscream was clearly very pleased with his idea.

At that moment, Soundwave interrupted his master with a series of loud *pings*, his face-visor displaying a radar map.

'What do you *mean* you can't pinpoint his signal?' Starscream turned on him. 'I know we are close! He's deep underground – boost the power to your sensors!' he commanded angrily.

As if he had been holding back until this point, Soundwave let out a new sound, and immediately a Decepticon emblem started flashing on the radar map.

Jabbing at his face-visor with a long, sharp, metal finger, Starscream nodded with satisfaction.

'Yes. *There.*'

Not wasting a second, both Decepticons immediately switched into jet mode and rocketed off down into the canyon below, heading in the direction of the life signal.

Raf smoothed a large piece of newspaper

over his new model volcano and separated another page from the stack on the floor. The black and yellow Autobot, Bumblebee, was beside him, bleeping away and gesturing with his arms as he chatted away to his human friend.

'Uh-huh. Uh-huh. Uh-huh,' Raf responded, listening carefully to every word whilst he worked away at his papier-mâché model.

He paused for a moment and looked steadily up at the Bot who, even crouched down, was many times bigger than him but not remotely scary in Raf's eyes.

'*Really*, Bumblebee? Then how *do* you make "warrior class"?'

Bumblebee bleeped and shrugged in reply.

'But I've seen you in action – you're *awesome*!'

Bumblebee looked down at the floor, obviously touched by his friend's remark, but also a little embarrassed. He didn't know that Optimus had entered their space until he felt his leader's large hand on his shoulder.

'I second your opinion, Raf,' Prime said warmly, 'but Autobot cycles are much longer than those of humans . . . and though it may be hard to believe, our young scout still has much to experience.'

Just then an alert sounded, causing all three of them to whip round and focus on the display panel on the wall, which Ratchet had been closely watching.

'Exposed Energon, and it's on the move,' Ratchet explained.

'And since *we* ain't moving it, guess who must be?' added Bulkhead, his colossal frame moving in next to Ratchet.

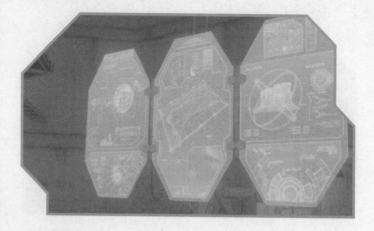

'*Decepticons*,' Arcee said decisively, joining the other Bots beside the grid map.

'Without Megatron?' Miko asked in amazement, coming forward to lean over the balcony above the display panel.

'Unfortunately, Megatron's *legacy* will live on, as others rise to take his place.' Optimus nodded wisely. His tone changed as he issued a command: 'Autobots, you have projects to complete.' He indicated the incomplete school projects. 'Ratchet,' he said decisively to the older Bot, 'I may require aid ...'

Ratchet, who had suddenly become absorbed in watching Raf work on his model volcano, was not so sure that this was the best decision. '"Science Fair" is a big part of their year,' he commented, having radically changed his attitude to the kids' school projects. 'Perhaps I'm better suited to remain behind and advise?'

Optimus took a moment and then nodded in agreement. 'Very well. Bumblebee, let us see about this Energon in transit.'

Bumblebee gathered himself and stood tall, ready for action.

The two Decepticons tugged hard at the huge stone coffin that was emerging from the rock wall in front of them, and finally the sarcophagus was free.

'Excellent, Soundwave.' For once, Starscream sounded pleased as his gaze lingered on the coffin that towered above them, its front carved with Cybertronian symbols. 'The Cube,' he said simply, holding out his hand as Soundwave opened the lid of a metal box and pulled out an Energon cube that glowed a brilliant turquoise.

Starscream wasted no time in feeding it into a square slot in the sarcophagus door. It slid in neatly and the Decepticon took a knowing step back, smiling.

'The Energon infusion – it's *working*!' he said as a blinding light shot out of it, causing them both to cower and cover their eyes.

At that moment, just round the corner there was a green whirl of shimmering light and Optimus and Bumblebee stepped from the GroundBridge portal, which immediately closed behind them, disappearing from sight once more.

The smaller Bot glanced around and let out a series of worried bleeps.

'No, Bumblebee, this does *not* look good,' agreed Prime. 'Hold your position, and await my command.'

Bumblebee watched anxiously as his leader strode away.

The lock on the coffin rotated and retreated, and as the door finally parted, Starscream stepped boldly forward.

'Awaken, warrior!' he exclaimed. 'Rise and serve your *new master*!'

A vast monster of a robot stepped out of the sarcophagus, dark green in colouring, its red eyes glowing with new energy as it slammed its fists together above its head. Then it bent almost double to speak face-to-face with Starscream, who stood a long way below.

'Skyquake serves only one master,' its huge voice rumbled.

'*Excellent*,' Starscream said with satisfaction. 'Your loyalty and devotion will set a fine example for the troops. No need to be timid, Skyquake. You may bow.'

'You fail to grasp my meaning.' The warrior spoke slowly but with force as he stood tall again. 'I am here on a mission assigned to me by my one master: Megatron.'

'Yes, him. Sadly, Megatron is no longer with us.' Starscream's voice was heavy with sarcasm.

'*Impossible*,' Skyquake said unbelievingly.

'And yet so. Very, very so. Your "one master" was obliterated.' Starscream spoke as if to a young child who was having trouble understanding. Then, with growing frustration, he continued, 'Why is this so difficult for everyone to accept?' He was quite angry now and took several steps towards the huge warrior as he made his final point. 'Skyquake, *I* located you. *I* awakened you. Thus, *I*, Lord Starscream, am now your master!'

Skyquake growled fiercely and advanced towards Starscream, his intention unmistakable . . .

Chapter Four

ANCIENT ORDERS

Starscream took a step backwards, desperate not to lose control but dwarfed by the colossal warrior.

Out of nowhere came a familiar voice.

'It has been a while, Skyquake.'

They both turned to see the Autobot leader step out from between two rocky outcrops.

On seeing Prime, Skyquake shoved Starscream roughly to one side and the Decepticon leader sighed with relief, never before so grateful to see his arch enemy.

Skyquake pulled himself up to his full height and faced the Autobot.

'*Optimus Prime.* I haven't seen you since the Battle of Technahar. Megatron ordered me to annihilate you.'

'That was a long time ago,' Optimus reminded him.

Bumblebee, who was hidden behind some rocks a little way off, watched his leader stride confidently forwards – focused on turning the situation into a peaceful one.

'That may be, Prime. *But my orders still stand,*' Skyquake replied threateningly.

Optimus stood his ground, determined to make his case.

'Is this ancient war still worth fighting,

when so many comrades have been lost and worlds destroyed?' he asked them both. Then, turning his attention to Starscream, he said a little more forcefully, 'Do you want to be a true leader, Starscream? Then stray from Megatron's path, and *lead the Decepticons towards peace.*'

Starscream paused for a moment as though seriously considering the idea. 'I would be willing to consider a truce ...' he answered politely, but then his smile turned into a sneer. 'If *you* would be willing to bow before me, Optimus Prime.'

Without waiting to hear Prime's

response, Skyquake exploded with rage.

'*Again?* Bow to THIS!' he raged, whacking Starscream and sending him hurtling into the rock wall, where the Deception leader slithered in a heap to the dusty ground.

Fearful for his life, Starscream staggered back to his feet and instantly switched into jet mode, shooting off into the sky above.

Optimus moved several steps closer to the Con warrior, a note of urgency in his voice as he made his appeal. 'Skyquake, this is a new era on a different world: side with the Autobots and help me end this conflict *for ever.*'

Skyquake shook his head. 'I will *never* side with a Prime!' he roared, running at the Autobot with outstretched arms.

He smashed Optimus into the rock wall, and then, picking him up by his shoulders, tossed him with all his might onto the canyon floor.

★

Soundwave was watching the battle from his vantage point high above, when Starscream jetted in and landed behind him on the rocky ridge.

The Decepticon shook himself and rubbed his leg where he had taken a blow, then strode towards Soundwave.

'What need have I for "peace",' he said in a mocking tone, 'when I have *Skyquake*?' Starscream's evil mind was already plotting his next move. 'With some discipline, he will *learn* to respect his new master . . .

'And,' he told Soundwave with absolute certainty, 'once it becomes known that Skyquake destroyed Optimus Prime under *my command*, all Decepticons will *gratefully* bow to me.'

Chapter Five

A NEW SIGNAL

From his hiding place, Bumblebee watched
with growing concern as Skyquake and
Optimus battled fiercely. He didn't know
what to do. His leader had ordered him to
stay put, but it was hard to stand by while
the Con warrior battled Prime. For now,
despite being the smaller of the two robots,
Optimus had the fight under control, so
Bumblebee decided to hang back, but he
was ready to jump in at any moment.

As his next move, the Autobot leader
switched his right arm into a gun, firing
out a shot that hit Skyquake squarely on
the chest, but bounced off his armour

plating without harming him. In response, Skyquake swiftly let off a series of high-energy blasts that all found their target, sending Optimus sliding backwards. The Autobot remained on his feet, but steam rose off his chest and he slumped forward from the impact.

Bumblebee had seen enough. He sprinted forward, barely registering Optimus' warning shout:

'Bumblebee, no!'

Leaping into the air, the yellow and black Autobot fired lasers from his fist, hitting Skyquake several times on the back. The shots merely pinged off him but they achieved their aim – he was distracted from Optimus. Instead, the warrior spun round and turned his gun on Bumblebee in a ferocious attack.

Still in the air by means of the small wings on his back, Bumblebee dodged the blasts, then flew bravely at Skyquake, but the enormous warrior grabbed him out of the air and hurled him into the rock face.

Seeing that Bumblebee was dazed and lying on the ground, Skyquake quickly lifted his gun, but he had not reckoned on Optimus' speed. With one decisive move, Prime pushed the Con's arm up into the air so that the shots fired uselessly into the sky.

By now, Bumblebee was back on his feet, and he ran full pelt at the warrior, but as the Autobot barged into him, Skyquake countered by throwing him with all his might onto the hard ground.

★

Meanwhile, up on the ridge, the whole battle was playing out on Soundwave's face visor as he recorded the action.

'Do not miss a single moment, Soundwave,' Starscream instructed him with obvious glee. 'We shall need visual proof of Optimus Prime's demise, for the historical record.'

Back down in the canyon gully, Skyquake was battering Optimus with a series of blows. The final punch sent him flying backwards and he landed next to Bumblebee, who was shaking off his daze from the heavy fall.

Picking himself up, Optimus saw that they had a few moments while the Con warrior was running through a weapons check. However, it looked as if he was preparing to charge them with a gun even bigger than the last, and although it was two against one, Prime knew that if he didn't think fast, the mighty Skyquake was going to make mincemeat of them. But what could the Autobots do to outsmart him . . . ? Suddenly, Optimus had it!

'Skyquake has not yet acquired a vehicle mode,' he told Bumblebee, just as the warrior let out a battle cry and started charging towards them. There was no time to lose.

'FALL BACK!' Optimus commanded, and in a split second the two robots had switched into vehicle mode.

As Skyquake reached them, Optimus and Bumblebee reversed, spun through 180 degrees and raced off at high speed, sending a huge dust cloud into the warrior's face.

'SO TIME HAS MADE YOU A COWARD, PRIME?' Skyquake roared, firing into the dirt after them.

'Now, where is it?' Ratchet mumbled to himself, sending sparks flying as his built-in arm welder made contact with the large metal model that he was working on. Since Optimus and Bumblebee's departure, he had done some serious work on the science projects.

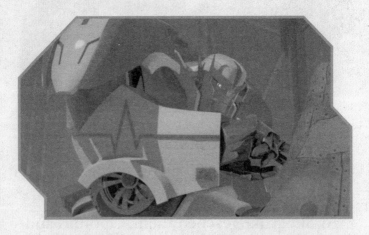

Raf was standing behind him, looking dumbfounded.

'Um, what *is* it?' he asked.

'You'll find out,' Ratchet replied, barely containing his excitement as he continued to weld.

'But Ratchet,' Raf challenged him as he walked between the Autobot's legs and timidly put out a hand to touch the model, 'if it's for school, shouldn't *I* be doing the work—'

Ratchet swiped the boy's hand away. 'Don't touch! Just watch . . . and *learn*,' he replied impatiently.

The Autobot crouched down in front of the metal object and got back to his welding, sending out a spray of blue sparks over Bulkhead and Arcee, who were sulkily watching the older Bot.

Bulkhead decided enough was enough, and spoke up above the noise of the welder: 'So, we'll just go and help Jack and Miko finish off their—'

'*Without my supervision?*' snapped Ratchet, jumping to his feet. 'You want their projects to be right, don't you?' he asked, turning off his arc-welder. Bulkhead and Arcee glanced at one another questioningly. Not pausing for their answer, Ratchet went on gleefully, '*Then watch a master at work.*' He switched the welder back on decisively.

Jack and Miko, who had also been watching glumly from the balcony above, exchanged glances.

'Control *frrreak*,' announced Miko. It looked like none of them had any say in the matter – it was going to be Ratchet's way, or no way at all.

'We've lost sight of them!' Starscream said angrily from the Decepticons' vantage point up on the ridge. 'Soundwave, why aren't you tracking them?' he demanded, noticing that Soundwave's face visor was displaying the empty canyon rather than a radar map.

Soundwave answered with a loud ping.

'What? What is it?' Starscream swung round in agitation. Then he noticed the radar map had popped up again and that something was flashing on it.

'A *second* Decepticon life-signal?' he said in surprise, turning away for a moment to think and tapping one of his long metal fingers impatiently on his arm. 'But Skyquake is the only "sleeper" buried in this area—'

Soundwave pinged again to indicate to Starscream to take a closer look.

This time the display was different – showing the Earth rotating slowly and then, out in space, the *Nemesis*. The Decepticon icon had appeared just a short distance away . . .

'The site of our *destroyed Spacebridge*?'

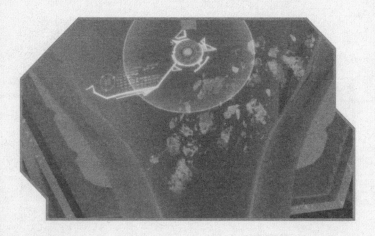

Starscream said in amazement.

He shook his head slowly and then his
eyes widened as he realized what this must
mean.

'You're not telling me' – he hesitated for
a moment, unable to voice what he knew
must be true – 'that life signal belongs to
Megatron?'

Chapter Six

BEARING WITNESS

In answer to his master's question, Soundwave switched the display on his face visor from the radar map to an image of a field of debris floating in space.

'B-but he was only *microns* from the detonation point,' Starscream stuttered in disbelief. 'Nothing could have survived that blast!'

He turned away from Soundwave again, still ranting at him and jabbing his finger in the air:

'Your sensors must be faulty! Ignore the contact, delete the coordinates—'

Soundwave stared blankly at his leader's

back, which was hunched over in rage, and pinged more loudly, displaying the radar map once again to prove that there was no mistake.

Starscream let out a breath of defeat and then checked himself. After all, he couldn't be seen to be *disappointed* that there was a chance the great Megatron still lived . . .

'What am I saying?' he said cheerily, forcing a smile as he swung back round to face Soundwave. 'Of course this must be investigated!' Dramatically, he flung an arm out and pointed up into the sky. 'If Lord Megatron is out there, I shall bring him home!'

Soundwave nodded in agreement and let out a series of beeps to indicate that he would assist Starscream in his search. However, the Decepticon leader had other ideas.

'Remain here and monitor the outcome,' he ordered. 'When Skyquake snuffs Prime's spark, I must bear witness.'

With that, Starscream swallow-dived off the ridge, only switching into jet-mode metres from the canyon floor. Then he rocketed back up into the sky, disappearing high in the clouds above.

Soundwave watched him go, replaying the Decepticon leader's last command on a loop: '*Must bear witness . . . Must bear witness . . .*' and then, without hesitation, the wing-shaped insignia on his chest dropped off, changing into the small jet 'Laserbeak' before shooting off in pursuit of Starscream.

Not far away, another jet was flying

the same skies, but at a much more leisurely pace. It was a military V-tol and Agent Fowler, the Autobot's designated government liaison, was in the cockpit.

'Tango-Six-Alpha to Central Command . . .' came a voice over the radio. Agent Fowler listened carefully. 'We're picking up Orbit-bound transmissions, originating from unidentified technology – possible hostile. We are moving to investigate.'

At that point, Fowler snapped into action, hitting the transmission button on the radio.

'Negative, Tango-Six-Alpha. This is Special Agent William Fowler, intercepting. Strike your report from the record, and provide origin coordinates,' he instructed, thrusting the V-tol up a gear and tearing through the sky. 'I'll take it from here.'

Chapter Seven

TAKING FLIGHT

Bumblebee, in his vehicle mode, careered round a tight corner of the rocky canyon at top speed. Skyquake charged after him, close on his tail. The ground shook with every step that the monstrous warrior took and his huge feet sent up dust clouds behind him.

Rounding another corner, Bumblebee was faced with a dead end. The craggy canyon wall stretched up high above him. He switched into robot mode and carried on running, turning his head to see his pursuer gaining on him. But there was no way out – he was trapped!

The Autobot stared up at the rock face, at a loss as to what to do next as Skyquake stormed in behind him.

'It will be a shame to crush you, bug,' said the Con warrior. 'But it is my duty.'

Yet Skyquake had barely spoken the words when a blaring horn distracted him. Headlights reflected on his armour plating as he whipped round to see Optimus in Big Rig mode, roaring towards him. With lightning reactions, Skyquake opened fire, but Optimus had already switched into robot mode and was running full pelt towards the warrior. He belted Skyquake with all his force, sending him flying into the rock face.

Righting himself, Optimus glanced over his shoulder at the other Autobot who now stood sheepishly behind him.

'Excellent strategy, Bumblebee!' Optimus said sarcastically.

Bumblebee looked away, embarrassed that he had got himself into such a tight spot.

Just then, Skyquake pulled himself out of the canyon wall where he had become embedded. He fell forward, rocks tumbling around him as his head slammed into the ground, forcing his eyes to close.

Bumblebee moved forward to join Optimus, when they were distracted by an aircraft jetting through the sky above them.

'Fowler?' said Optimus, recognizing the V–tol.

Behind them, Skyquake opened his eyes. He immediately spotted the jet plane and, seeing an opportunity, smiled to himself as he shot out two powerful scanning beams

from his eyes, which zoomed into the sky
and locked onto the aircraft.

Optimus reacted quickly and, pressing the
comm-link in the side of his head, spoke
urgently to the human.

'Agent Fowler, fall back!'

Up in the cockpit, the pale blue light of
the scanning beams washed over Fowler,
taking him by surprise. The next thing he
was aware of was a painful electric shock in
his hands, causing him to drop the controls.

'*Argh!*' he cried out, examining his hands.

Down below, a technical image of the
V-tol was being displayed in each of

Skyquake's eyes, as though a complex calculation was going on. Then the Con Warrior smiled with satisfaction, closed his eyes and quickly rose to his feet. Before the Autobots knew what was happening, Skyquake began to charge at Optimus, but then he leaped in the air, rapidly changing into a replica V-tol and rocketing off into the sky above, leaving smoke trails in his wake.

In seconds, he had cleared the clouds and was in the air space above Fowler.

The agent was astonished at the sight of a jet plane identical to his in every way, apart from colouring and a strange insignia. Fowler's military plane was dark grey all over, whereas this intruder aircraft was dark green with red tips.

'Well, I'll be a bald eagle . . .' Agent Fowler said out loud as the alien V-tol zoomed off.

'Air superiority *achieved*,' Skyquake

announced to himself as he looped round and headed back in the direction of the canyon labyrinth in search of the Autobots.

Gaining them in his sights, Skyquake opened fire, tearing up the canyon floor.

Optimus and Bumblebee turned and ran, switching into their vehicle modes to gain maximum speed and dodge the stream of bullets that rained down on them.

Skyquake flew low, navigating the twists and turns of the labyrinth. He was gaining on the Autobots and, fixing a lock on Bumblebee, he opened his undercarriage in one swift movement to reveal two heat-seeker missiles.

Rat-tat-tat-tat-tat!

Skyquake was being hit from behind by pulse blasts from Fowler's plane.

'Stealing plans for a classified military aircraft will not be tolerated on my watch!' Fowler cried.

But then the alien aircraft pulled back, looping round so that it had the rear position and, to Fowler's astonishment, released six fast-moving missiles.

He reacted swiftly, zooming away, and flying low into the labyrinth, but the missiles were locked on to him. Puzzled, Fowler read his radar.

'Heat-seeking missiles? But my plane doesn't have those!'

So, it wasn't just in colouring that this V-tol was different to his, after all. But there was no time to think. He raced round the next corner, the missiles gaining on him as he found himself heading for a dead end . . .

Seeing his opportunity, Fowler flew directly at the canyon rock face ahead of him . . . and then, at the last moment, shot vertically into the sky. All six missiles smashed into the canyon wall and exploded.

'I've still got it!' Fowler said with pride as he zoomed off.

Chapter Eight

DEEP SPACE

Unrecognizable chunks of blackened, twisted metal floated amongst a never-ending carpet of twinkling stars. It was the debris field from the ruined Spacebridge, which had exploded and blown apart, yet still hung in a loose cluster in its ruined state, the lack of gravity not letting each part go its separate way. From out of the purple-black landscape of surrounding space, a sleek jet zoomed in.

Switching back into robot mode, Starscream dropped down, landing neatly on one of the larger pieces of rubble. 'No one could have survived this,' he said nervously, wanting it to be true. As he looked around at the total and utter devastation, he became convinced that nothing could have escaped in one piece.

'As I suspected: faulty sensors,' he said with confidence. He stroked his pointed chin with a long metal finger, deep in thought. 'The last thing I need now is rumours that Megatron is still—'

A strange sound interrupted him. It sounded like a moan of pain.

Starscream gasped.

Then, swiftly, he began leaping from one chunk of rubble to the next, searching out the source of the noise. Until he spotted what looked like a robot drifting limply in space . . .

'Megatron!'

Starscream couldn't believe his eyes. There before him was the battered body of his former master. Badly singed and with a crater in his chest, but still in one piece.

He placed his hands on the lifeless form,

and the head suddenly sprang forward, Megatron's red eyes glowing wildly as he growled and then slumped back again.

'But how . . . ?'

Starscream could not believe it possible, yet when he peered into the gaping hole in Megatron's chest he saw that there was a fragment of purple crystal there, still glowing brightly.

'*Dark Energon. Of course . . .*' he said, recognizing the precious life source that had powered Megatron's undead Terrorcon army.

He leaned his face close to his master's

and whispered: 'Everyone believes you are deceased. Who am I to disappoint them?'

An evil smile played on his lips as he reached into Megatron's damaged spark chamber and grasped the shard of Dark Energon. As he pulled it out, Megatron groaned and his red eyes flickered for a moment before going dark. He fell back once more.

Still holding the precious purple crystal, Starscream was about to retreat when a movement caught his eye.

It was Laserbeak.

As the small Decepticon jet approached,

Starscream hid the Dark Energon behind his back, thinking fast.

Once more, grasping Megatron's shoulders, he spoke loudly to Laserbeak.

'Soundwave, if you are listening, I have found Lord Megatron and he is . . . unwell,' he reported, his voice thick with concern.

'We must transport him to the sickbay, *immediately*!' Starscream ordered, his hand tightly clasping the shard of Dark Energon behind his back, hidden from Laserbeak's view.

Chapter Nine

THE CHASE

The Big Rig and muscle car skidded at top speed through the narrow gully, only just keeping ahead of the Decepticon V-tol. Yet another one of his missiles exploded into the canyon wall, sending rocks tumbling down behind the Autobots as they accelerated away. But within seconds, Skyquake was flying over them and, fixing Optimus in his sights, he dispatched a cannon blast that only narrowly missed the Big Rig's rear end, sending the blue and red truck skidding on its side.

Prime reacted fast and switched back to robot mode to right himself, then half sprinted, half stumbled away, expecting a full-on attack from the Con warrior. But instead, Skyquake jetted off in pursuit of Bumblebee, flying down low over him and firing rapidly, before zooming off ahead to loop back round and finish him off.

They had reached the end of the gully and Bumblebee, in muscle car mode, was heading up an incline which appeared to drop away to nothing. As his wheels hit the edge, he flew up into the air and then, switching modes as he fell, landed on the ledge and started running as soon as his robotic feet hit the ground. He kept his eyes firmly on the alien aircraft which was looping round in the canyon and coming back to find him and Optimus.

As it circled in below, Bumblebee took a flying leap off the ledge and threw himself at the green and red V-tol, catching onto a wing as it careered past him.

The jet plane faltered under his weight for a moment, and then, realizing he had an uninvited Autobot onboard, Skyquake immediately set about trying to rid himself of his unwanted passenger.

His first move was to fly sideways, right up against the canyon wall, in a bid to scrape Bumblebee off his wing. There was an ear-splitting scraping sound and sparks flew off the Autobot's back as his metal plating made contact with the rock face, but Bumblebee held fast.

Then Skyquake turned his nose skyward and rocketed vertically upwards at top speed, his passenger still clinging on for dear life . . .

All Optimus could do from the ground was watch helplessly. Then, realizing that Agent Fowler was somewhere out there still, Prime spoke to him urgently on the comm-link.

'Agent Fowler, we require immediate assistance.'

Meanwhile, Skyquake, having failed to rid himself of Bumblebee, changed tactic and flipped over to fly upside down. The sudden movement swung the Autobot off the wing but he clung on, his body hanging dangerously in mid-air. The fight had not gone out of Bumblebee, and with sheer determination, he swung his huge yellow and black body up and landed on the top of the plane. Sitting astride the V-tol and steadying himself with one hand, he used his other fist to hammer at the aircraft's metal casing until he had succeeded in breaking through the fuselage.

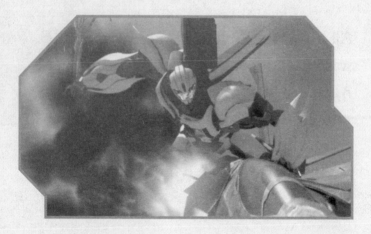

The Autobot began ripping out wires and parts until the jet burst into flames and immediately began to nosedive headlong towards the ground . . .

★

Thick black smoke poured out of the back of the alien aircraft as Agent Fowler's jet tore through the sky towards it. He drew level with the plummeting V-tol, both of them hurtling towards the canyon floor.

The Autobot shifted his frame into a crouching position, readied himself for the jump, and took an almighty leap into the air.

Without his extra weight, the alien V-tol fell even faster, and as Bumblebee made a successful landing on top of Fowler's plane, the military jet dipped at first before Fowler righted it and flew back up into the sky, clear of danger.

Optimus had watched Fowler's rescue mission with huge relief, and now kept his eye trained on the burning V-tol as it ripped through the sky and hit the hard ground close by him. He was confident that even Skyquake could not have survived the crash, but he needed to check it out with his own eyes . . .

'Happy landings, Con,' said Fowler with satisfaction, flying over to a ridge so that his passenger could hop off safely.

Bumblebee ran to the edge just as Prime reached Skyquake, and leaped down to join his leader.

'Had Skyquake chosen to stray from his master's path, we might not be burying him today,' Optimus said sombrely.

The two of them stood in silence next to the smoking remains.

Up on the ridge, Soundwave's recording mechanism whirred.

Chapter Ten

MARKS OUT OF TEN

Dusk had settled on the Nevada desert and all was quiet. The vast stretch of sand looked grey in the dim light, as did the outline of Outpost Omega One, the Autobots' secret headquarters, hidden in the landscape of rocky outcrops.

Deep underground, Ratchet was putting the finishing touches to cleaning up Bumblebee. The yellow and black Autobot was inside a glass chamber a short distance away that housed various lasers which Ratchet was controlling with a lever in each hand.

'Bumblebee,' said Optimus, who had

been watching his friend being repaired, 'putting *yourself* at risk was perhaps not the wisest strategy . . .'

Bumblebee bleeped his apology as the door to the glass chamber slid open and he stepped out.

'But you performed admirably,' Optimus went on, his voice full of pride as the young scout emerged, looking as good as new.

Just then, they were interrupted by the sound of engines and a horn blaring and the doors to the exit tunnel slid open as Bulkhead and Arcee rolled in.

'Ah-ha-ha-ha – there you are!' Ratchet said in excitement, hurrying over as Bulkhead's doors opened. Raf and Miko jumped out and Jack dismounted from the motorbike.

'Well?' he said impatiently. 'How were my – er, *our* school projects received?'

The two teenagers exchanged awkward glances with Raf, who spoke up:

'Well . . .'

Miko's mobile was hanging from a stand that she had placed on the teacher's desk. It held a strange-looking planet made up of unrecognizable black, orange and turquoise techy swirls with a small similar-looking 'moon' on either side. The Japanese girl stood next to it, looking uncertain.

'Miss Makadi, what planet would that be?' came the teacher's voice.

'Er . . . Cybertron,' Miko replied apologetically, just as the cord holding the planet snapped and the big metal ball smashed onto the desk . . .

Meanwhile, in another classroom, Jack stood nervously next to his 'motorbike engine'.

'It's certainly . . . large, Mr Darby . . . but does it work?' asked his teacher.

Jack crouched down by the alien-looking engine and cautiously flicked a switch. The machine leaped into life and started jumping randomly about the classroom, causing the pupils and teacher to scream in panic. Then it rammed into the classroom door, knocking it off its hinges, and disappeared out into the corridor . . .

In Raf's classroom, the big welded metal 'volcano' sat in the middle of the floor in front *of the blackboard in place of the teacher's desk. It was taller than Raf, who stood anxiously next to it, not appearing to be very proud of this strange model with its red and green buttons on the front and blue currents of electricity crackling all over it.*

'I hate to ask, Mr Esquivel – but is it active . . . ?'

Raf responded to the teacher's question by taking a step back, closing his eyes tightly, and pressing a button on the remote he had been holding.

The volcano fired a blinding energy beam out of its crater, which shot up through the ceiling and out through the roof of the school . . .

Once the kids had finished describing how 'their' projects had been received, all three of them stood at the feet of Arcee and Bulkhead, glaring angrily at Ratchet.

'Well, on our planet you would have been awarded the highest honours,' Ratchet grumbled, before stomping away and muttering to himself.

Bumblebee came over and looked up at the Autobot leader, bleeping out his opinion.

'Indeed, Bumblebee,' Optimus agreed. 'Our human friends would have been wise to stray from Ratchet's path.'

His answer was good-humoured but his meaning was clear. It is not always right to blindly follow someone who declares himself to be a 'master' – sometimes the best course of action is to trust your instincts and use your own judgement, just as Bumblebee had demonstrated that day.

★

Up in space, the *Nemesis* spaceship moved slowly through the star-studded sky.

On board, in the laboratory, Starscream was talking to Soundwave.

They stood before an angled metal trolley on which Megatron lay – unconscious but breathing. Plugged into him were several thick cables leading to nearby machines that beeped and pumped, keeping him alive.

'The troops will be pleased to hear of our success in rushing Lord Megatron into stasis,' Starscream said to his fellow Decepticon. He was saying the words that he knew Soundwave wanted to hear, but it was obvious from his expression that he felt just the opposite.

'Let us hope that our Master pulls through,' he continued, barely able to disguise the bitter snarl that curled his mouth.

As ever, Soundwave said nothing, taking it all in, and filing it away for the record.

TRANS FORMERS

P R I M E

OFF THE RAILS

Chapter One

THE DINGUS

'Prime!'

'*Prime!*'

'Special Agent Fowler?' responded Optimus Prime as he strode towards the monitor in the control room that displayed a live feed of Fowler sitting in the cockpit of his grounded V-tol jet, shouting for the Autobot leader. 'To what do we owe—' Optimus continued, joining Ratchet in front of the wall-mounted screen. But Agent Fowler interrupted him, not interested in exchanging pleasantries.

'What else? Cons.'

Fowler was the Autobots' government

liaison officer, and he had a direct communication link with their headquarters. The Autobot HQ was located in an empty missile base in the Nevada desert. Apart from the Autobots, only Fowler, and the Bots' three young friends – Raf, Jack and Miko – knew of its whereabouts.

'I chased them off, but not before they blew me out of the sky!' Fowler explained as the monitor picture flicked over to show the military jet stuck in a churned-up ditch on the outskirts of a forest. The jet had smoke trails coming off it and looked in bad shape from its crash landing.

'*Again?*' snickered the Japanese girl, Miko, who was watching the scene play out from a viewing balcony. Standing on either side of her were the boys – twelve-year-old Raf and fifteen-year-old Jack.

'They tried a "smash 'n' grab" for the Dingus,' Fowler went on, looking none too pleased.

'The *whatsit?*' asked the slim female Autobot, Arcee, raising an eyebrow in surprise.

'Dynamic Nuclear Generation System: aka *Dingus*,' Fowler explained, pushing a button in his cockpit that switched over the picture on the monitor again. Now it displayed the contents of the jet's hold, which was a metal crate with nuclear warning symbols on it, secured by straps that were bolted into the floor. 'It's a prototype energy source I'm transporting to the coast for testing,' the agent continued grumpily.

'That's absurd,' scoffed Ratchet, talking over the comm-link. 'Why would Starscream bother with such primitive technology?'

'I'm guessing to make a big fat primitive weapon of mass destruction,' Fowler said defensively. 'If this baby were to melt down it would irradiate this state and the four next door.' The big man leaned into the camera. He was clearly getting a bit fed up that the Autobots were not seeing the situation for what it was – highly dangerous.

All three of the kids looked at each other in alarm. Raf gulped.

'Er, did Agent Fowler say which state he's in?' he asked nervously.

Fowler decided it was time to spell things out. 'I'm a sitting duck here, Prime,' he said, wagging a finger at the camera to make his point. 'I need *you* to spin up your GroundBridge and send the Dingus to its destination before the Cons come back for it.'

'I'm afraid that sending such a volatile device through the GroundBridge is out of the question.' Optimus leaned in closer to the monitor, his voice grave. 'If there were to be an accident during its transmission, the radiation of which you speak could multiply through the GroundBridge vortex and harm all *fifty* states and beyond.'

Agent Fowler took in the full impact of what the Autobot leader was telling him but he was at a loss. The fight had gone out of him and he looked deflated. He had been relying upon the Bots nipping in with their special 'Bridge' that created a portal anywhere on Earth, and transported whatever was in it to wherever they instructed it to go. How else were they going to get the Dingus safely out of there?

'You got any better ideas?' he asked desperately.

Chapter Two

ON THE ROAD

Agent Fowler rubbed his hands together and placed them on the steering wheel of the enormous blue and red Big Rig.

'No need, Agent Fowler,' came Optimus Prime's voice. 'I will handle the driving.'

Fowler, who was sitting in the driver's seat of the Big Rig's cab, had been looking forward to taking command of the powerful vehicle. Now he crossed his arms grumpily, and sat back in his seat. 'It's gonna be a long trip . . .' he muttered.

Optimus started his engine. Bulkhead and Bumblebee, who were parked next to him in the clearing, did the same.

'Autobots – roll out,' Optimus ordered, and the convoy, with the Dingus safely stowed in a trailer attached to the back of the Big Rig, set off.

They were driving down a long straight road, with forest on either side, heading for the foothills of the Rocky Mountains. Optimus was at the front, with Bumblebee behind him, and Bulkhead bringing up the rear.

Back at base, Ratchet was monitoring their progress.

'We're locked onto your coordinates, Optimus,' he said, watching three moving flashing lights on the communications console. Miko, Jack and Raf were there with him, tracking the convoy's progress. 'Barring any complications, you should reach the drop-off point by sundown,' he went on confidently.

Miko yawned – without Bulkhead around, there was not much fun going down at the Autobots' headquarters.

Optimus was moving at a steady pace and there were not many cars on the road, but now he had come up behind an old truck that was barely crawling along.

Fowler blasted the horn a couple of times, and when there was no response from the truck he leaned on it – hard.

'Move it, Grandpa!' he said, whacking the steering-wheel in frustration.

His actions had the desired effect and the truck pulled off the road to let the convoy pass. Fowler gave the horn a final blast.

'Agent Fowler, is that really necessary?'
Optimus asked in an even voice.

'Aw, don't tell me you're one of those
textbook drivers?' the agent said, rolling his
eyes and slumping back in his seat.

'They're transporting it in an unarmed
civilian truck?' said a voice. It came
from a helicopter flying just behind the
convoy, keeping a close eye on them.
He watched as the yellow and black car
pulled out into the opposite lane and
took the lead.

'Send in the ground units,' the voice

commanded, making a decision.

'You know, you're saving my bacon here, Prime,' Fowler said conversationally, one hand on the wheel, and an arm resting on the window as he watched the landscape slide by.

'I'm glad to be of service, Agent Fowler,' Optimus replied.

'Of course, it's not like I'd *need* your help if you and the Cons had stuck to tearing up your *own* corner of the Galaxy . . .' Fowler said, a little spikily.

'Are you suggesting that no evil existed on your world before we arrived?' asked Prime patiently.

'Well . . .' Fowler responded, realizing the Autobot had a point. 'It was, er, a *different* evil . . .' The agent wanted to change the subject now, aware that he had lost that debate. 'How about some radio?' he suggested. 'You seem like a "Nashville sound" kind of guy.' But before Optimus could answer him, Fowler was alerted to the sound of a helicopter, and looking in the Big Rig's wing mirror he saw that a chopper was trailing them.

'That's it! That's the Con that shot me down . . .' he reported. 'Who is he?' he demanded. 'Wingnut? Dingbat? Skyguy?'

Before Optimus could respond, Bulkhead's voice came over the walkie-talkie that was lying on the passenger seat.

'Watch your rear-view,' he warned as three high-tech racing cars drove up behind him.

'Feeling a little constricted without the use of my fists here, boss,' Bulkhead complained as two of the identical green and black racing cars positioned themselves on either side of him.

'Remain in vehicle mode unless absolutely necessary,' Optimus told him firmly.

The third car pulled out in front of Bulkhead. Fowler was watching the action closely in the Big Rig's mirrors.

'A whole team of Cons!' he exclaimed.
'What?' asked Ratchet over the comm-
link. 'I'm not picking up anything,' he went
on, puzzled at the absence of any new
movement on his radar. 'They must be
using a new cloaking technology.'

At that moment a fourth and fifth car
appeared, and one of them accelerated to
the front of the convoy, sliding in ahead of
Bumblebee. The muscle car responded by
pulling into the opposite lane, but the high-
tech car mirrored his move, not letting
him pass.

The other car then drew up alongside the Big Rig's cab and Agent Fowler watched as the sunroof slid back . . . Inside was not a Decepticon, but a masked gunman! The assailant stood up and pointed his gun directly at Fowler.

'Pull over!' he growled.

'Well, I'll be dipped!' said Agent Fowler in surprise.

'Our assailants are not Decepticons – they are human,' Optimus announced over the comm-link.

'*Human?*' Jack, Raf and Ratchet all said in unison, when they heard the news.

'Oh, *please*, taking on our Bots?' said Miko in a mocking tone. 'They're road kill!' she finished enthusiastically, waving a fist at the screen.

'Gentlemen,' said the head of the operation, who was surveying the scene from up in the helicopter. 'Stop their engines.'

In response, the masked man fired at Fowler, but Optimus swerved and the sonic blast exploded harmlessly on the road behind the trailer.

'Who *are* these guys?' asked Fowler, beginning to feel worried.

'Autobots, maintain your cover and apply minimal force . . . disarm them only,' Prime instructed the others.

At that moment, the car with the gunman in, which had hung back after the unsuccessful pop at Fowler, sped forwards again and the marksman aimed at Bumblebee. But the Autobot was too nifty for them and reversed into the green and black car a couple of times, then shunted it sideways. The assailants' car skidded back into a rock by the side of the road and the driver lost control, causing the vehicle to flip over onto its roof.

Up in the air, the commander – Silas – who had been observing the action from the chopper, glanced at the pilot and shook his head. 'Those are *not* civilian drivers.'

Chapter Three

MECH

The road was climbing higher and higher in the mountains now. Down on the left was a steep drop-off, only broken by the pine trees that carpeted the valley below.

The Autobot convoy had broken away from the high-tech cars and was careering round the corners in a bid to gain some distance. Agent Fowler was beginning to feel pretty sick from being thrown around in the Big Rig's cab.

'I could use some air,' he said weakly.

Prime rolled down a window and Fowler leaned his head out and gazed into the wing mirror. He could hear the chopper overhead and saw that the pursuing cars had kept close on their tail.

Just then, one of the sleek racing cars pulled up beside Optimus and another masked man leaped from its roof onto the trailer with a laser gun in his hand. Immediately he started working on detaching the trailer from the Big Rig.

'Optimus, bear right!' Fowler called out urgently.

Optimus responded immediately and, with a screeching of tyres, swung right, causing the intruder to lose balance and lurch out into the road, but he hung on with one hand and steadied himself. The Big Rig veered again, this time hitting the car, sending it flying off the road. The car flipped over and landed on its roof on a protruding ledge below. Its driver crawled out unharmed, but the car was totalled.

Meanwhile, Fowler, seeing that the masked man was still busy with the laser gun on the trailer, jumped out of the cab and edged himself carefully along the cabin step. Then he reached in, grabbing the imposter by the back of his jacket, and dangled him out over the road, sending the laser gun flying.

'You're gonna tell me everything I wanna kno—' Fowler's interrogation technique was cut short by a passing branch that whipped the man out of his grasp . . .

Agent Fowler glanced at his empty hands in disbelief and then scrambled back into the cab and belted himself in.

Immediately, the walkie-talkie on the passenger seat crackled into life:

'I do hope you take better care of the Dingus than you do of your captives.'

Puzzled, Fowler picked up the walkie-talkie and then, as he heard the chopper approaching, figured out where the voice was coming from.

'This is Special Agent William Fowler here – identify yourself!' he said angrily.

'I am Silas. But of greater consequence to you, *WE* are . . . MECH,' came the steely reply. 'Fair warning – we will be helping ourselves to your device, even if it means inflicting casualties,' he continued.

The hard voice belonged to the

commander up in the chopper – a large man with close-cropped grey hair and long red scars running over his face. He looked as if he was not afraid of a brawl. But then, neither was Fowler.

'Is that so?' Agent Fowler replied sarcastically. 'Tell me, *Sy* – what's the market price for a Dingus these days?'

'What makes you think we intend to *sell* it, Agent Fowler?' Silas replied with some menace.

Fowler glanced down at the walkie-talkie in his hand and then up at the chopper. The message was clear – MECH was not in it for the money, but for the power they would gain if they got their hands on a device capable of such complete and utter mass destruction.

Chapter Four

HIDDEN WEAPON

'There's a war brewing,' the MECH commander explained, 'between the new world order and the *newest* world order.' Silas's voice had taken on a sinister edge. 'The victor will be the side armed with the most innovative technology.'

Fowler listened, but at the same time he was watching closely in the Big Rig's wing mirror at what was going on behind them.

One of the four MECH cars that had Bulkhead boxed in had pulled up closer to the trailer and another masked gunman was standing up out of the sun-roof. He held a device that looked like a gun, but when he fired it, three discs with metal spikes in them shot out and attached themselves to the door of the trailer. Then he pushed another button on the side of the strange gun, which caused the discs to imbed themselves further into the door, emitting a powerful electric charge between the three of them, followed by a small explosion. This released the three-part locking device on the trailer and then the door slid up.

Fowler had remained silent throughout this procedure, but as the gunman climbed forward onto the bonnet of the MECH car and prepared to launch himself onto the trailer, he spoke up.

'So, Sy – you think MECH has all of
the most advanced tech?' he asked in a
voice that was almost gleeful. He smirked
as Arcee came flying out of the back of
the trailer at top speed and crashed down
onto the bonnet of the MECH car, sending
the gunman hurtling over the back of it,
yowling in pain.

The impact of her landing caused the car
to spin round, then flip over and hit the
MECH car behind, which in turn flipped
through one hundred and eighty degrees,
and hit the tarmac roof-side down.

Bulkhead was finally free of his entourage, and the Autobots stepped their speed up a notch.

As the chopper flew down to inspect the scene, the pilot shook his head. 'Definitely not civilian drivers,' he commented to Silas.

'Laters, Sy,' Fowler said smugly into the walkie-talkie, smiling with satisfaction.

As the Big Rig accelerated away, Optimus had a few words to say on the matter.

'Agent Fowler – do not take Silas lightly,' he warned. 'Megatron preached the very same ideas before plunging Cybertron into the Great War that destroyed our world,' he added gravely.

The agent frowned, but then Ratchet's voice interrupted his thoughts.

'Optimus – prepare to initiate phase two. Five miles ahead to the south you will reach the rendezvous point,' he told his leader.

For now, they had to concentrate on the

mission in hand – ensuring the safe passage of the Dingus.

Far up in the clouds above, an evil-looking spacecraft was hovering.

It was the *Nemesis* – the Decepticon spaceship.

'*Five miles ahead to the south, you will reach the rendezvous point . . .*'

Onboard, Soundwave was broadcasting a sound-recording of Ratchet's speech to his leader.

When his face-visor, which had been displaying a voice-recognition pattern, had gone blank, Starscream leaned in and spoke, his red eyes narrowing.

'And, so . . . the Autobots are outside the confines of their base and sound otherwise engaged,' he commented. He turned away, plotting. 'Which means they will never see us coming . . . Find them!' he ordered the six troopers, who were standing to attention, awaiting his command. 'And

SCRAP THEM!' Starscream bellowed, closing his hand into a fist as if squashing a mere insect.

'Yes, Lord Starscream,' the troops answered in unison, each of them raising their right hand diagonally across their chest in a salute of loyalty.

Starscream smiled at the sight and chuckled to himself.

Chapter Five

PHASE TWO

The road that the Autobot convoy was travelling along was twisting its way through the valley now, with a railway track sunken down beside it. Bumblebee drove ahead of Optimus; Arcee rode next to the truck and trailer, and Bulkhead brought up the rear. The Autobots knew that the remaining three MECH cars were not far behind.

As they rounded the next corner, Fowler indicated the two tunnels cut in the rock face a couple of hundred metres ahead of them – one for cars, and a wider one for trains to pass through.

'There's our destination point,' he said.

With no time to lose, Optimus spoke to the others: 'Autobots – keep a tight formation!'

In response, Arcee swerved across the Big Rig's path, then turned sharply and accelerated, taking off high into the air and jumping the bank that ran down to the railway track!

Moments later, Optimus, Bumblebee and Bulkhead veered off the road, and headed at full speed down the steep grassy verge onto the rough ground that ran alongside the track. Then the four Autobot vehicles raced into the tunnel, neck-and-neck with a freight train, just as the MECH cars began to descend the bank in hot pursuit.

Bulkhead, still at the rear, suddenly spun round and switched into robot mode, shooting huge sonic blasts out of both arms into the roof of the mouth of the tunnel. Just as the MECH cars were about to career through the entrance, a huge shower of rocks tumbled down, blocking their path and causing them to skid to a halt. Satisfied with his work, Bulkhead changed back into vehicle mode and sped off to catch up with the others.

Optimus was still driving parallel to the train, with Bumblebee and Bulkhead close behind. Suddenly, Bumblebee switched into robot mode, ran a couple of strides and then leaped onto the roof of the moving train, where he leaned over and rapped on the door of one of the cargo cars . . .

'Tactical error,' said Silas smugly as the chopper flew over the crumbled tunnel. 'There's only one way out,' he added, watching both the train and the Autobot convoy emerge from the other end of the tunnel.

He smiled to himself, thinking the Dingus would soon be in his possession, when he was distracted by a sound close by. Looking out of his window, he was

surprised to see a strange purple aircraft
flying parallel to the chopper for a moment,

before it – and five other identical jets –
rocketed away.

Down on the ground, Fowler too had
spotted the jets.

'Air support?' he wondered out loud,
leaning out of the Big Rig's window. 'Ours
or theirs?' he asked.

'Optimus,' came Ratchet's voice in
response. 'You have company!' he warned
as the six Decepticon aircraft showed up on
his radar map.

At that moment the Cons released a shower of missiles and then looped away as the warheads headed in the direction of the Autobot convoy.

'It must be the military!' said Silas. 'But firing on their *own* agents?' He and his pilot could not believe what they were seeing.

Meanwhile, Optimus was swerving about to dodge the missiles, sending his wheel spinning.

'Ohhh,' cried out Fowler as he was thrown about the cab.

In response to the jerking movement of the truck, the damaged trailer gave way and broke free of the Big Rig, smashing down onto the road, just as one of the missiles made contact with the tarmac . . .

'Sir – the Dingus!' Silas's pilot panicked.

The Autobots raced off as the missile exploded in an almighty blast that engulfed the whole road, sending the trailer flying up into the air in bits.

The pilot, who had been frantically watching his monitor, breathed out.

'Sir . . . I'm not reading any radiation,' he informed his boss with relief. 'The Dingus didn't melt down . . .' he said in surprise.

'No . . . *it did not* . . .' Silas replied slowly as the truth began to dawn on him.

Chapter Six

DROPPING COVER

By now, the Autobot convoy had come off the road and entered a clearing. Each of the Decepticon jets which had flown in overhead now changed into robot mode and dropped from the sky.

The clearing ended with a low wall that dropped off to a steep incline and the Bots, arriving at this dead end, skidded to a halt, turning as they stopped to find themselves trapped by six advancing Decepticon troopers.

'Agent Fowler,' Optimus said, 'We have no choice. I'm afraid that if you *and* we are to survive . . . it has become absolutely necessary to drop our cover.'

The human had only a split second to think about what this meant, because in the next moment the Big Rig and his companions had switched into robot mode.

Optimus stood up, with Agent Fowler in the palm of his hand, retching from the sudden movement.

He was not the only human to be surprised by the unexpected transformation. Silas had not been prepared for what he saw in the clearing as his chopper hovered overhead. However, it did not come as a huge shock to him – he had been aware that there was something extraordinary about whoever was operating the vehicles he had been chasing . . .

'So, the rumours *are* true,' he said to his pilot, sounding a little amused. '*Living* technology stands before us . . . though perhaps not for very long.' He chuckled as the chopper looped away.

Meanwhile, Optimus had placed Fowler

up on a high ledge, out of harm's way.

'Remain here,' he instructed him.

'Will do,' replied Agent Fowler, glancing at the big drop behind him.

The Autobots strode towards the Decepticon troopers, Bulkhead at the front.

'After a long road trip, it feels good to get out of the car,' he said cheerily, 'stretch my legs, and KICK SOME TAIL PIPE!' He roared and smashed his enormous fists together.

With that, the four Autobots ran towards the approaching Decepticons and the battle began . . .

★

From his vantage point in the chopper, which the pilot was circling over the clearing, Silas could not tear his eyes away from the fighting robots. They were ducking and diving and throwing punches, just as brawling men would, although their size and strength was so much greater and the blows much more damaging. He could see that the ones he had been pursuing on the road appeared to be swifter and more tactical in their moves than the six identical purple robots. It was fascinating to watch—

'Sir?' The pilot's voice interrupted his thoughts. 'If the Dingus wasn't in the truck—'

'Yes. Indeed,' he responded, pressing a button on his comm-link. 'Special Agent Fowler,' he said. 'You lead a charmed life, walking among Titans.'

Fowler retrieved the walkie-talkie from his suit pocket and put it to his ear. He looked up at the chopper in the sky.

'Come on down,' he invited Silas. 'I'll introduce you.'

'In good time.' Silas smiled as he glanced down at his radar map. 'But at the moment I'm wondering how the Dingus might have vanished into thin air without a trace ...' On the screen a purple light was flashing and moving steadily along a green line that looked remarkably like a train track.

Fowler's eyes widened in alarm. Was Silas on to them? He cast his mind back to what had taken place in the railway tunnel:

When Bumblebee had rapped on the side of the cargo car, the door slid back to reveal a soldier inside. The yellow and black robot waved in greeting. Then the sides of Optimus' Big Rig trailer collapsed to reveal Arcee crouched on its floor, next to the Dingus. Carefully, she lifted the precious box and handed it to Bulkhead, who was also holding onto the side of the freight train in robot mode. He then passed it over to Bumblebee, who slotted it in through the door of the cargo train and placed it at the soldier's feet.

All in the few seconds before the train and the convoy emerged into view from the tunnel . . .

'Now, if you'll excuse me' – Silas's voice came over the walkie-talkie and confirmed Fowler's fear – 'I have a train to catch.'

Agent Fowler watched in alarm as the chopper turned and flew away, rapidly disappearing from sight.

'Prime!' Fowler spoke urgently into the walkie-talkie, alerting the Autobot leader, who was exchanging savage blows with two of the troopers beside the ledge of the drop-off. 'Silas got wise to phase two!'

'I understand,' responded Optimus,

glancing over at the agent and taking his eyes off his opponents.

The lapse in concentration cost him dearly, as in the next moment one of the Con troopers smashed an entire tree trunk into his face.

Catching him off guard, Optimus went flying backwards and over the edge of the cliff, where he smashed down on the rocks below . . .

Landing face down, he lifted his head for a moment, but the effort was almost too much for him.

'Prime! Do you read me?' Fowler shouted urgently into the walkie-talkie. 'Prime!'

The Autobot leader groaned and slumped back down onto the rocks. His eyes closed.

Chapter Seven

PHASE THREE

In the clearing, the battle was still raging and three of the Decepticon troopers had just charged Bulkhead all at once. Now that they were down to three against six, the Autobots really had their hands full.

Back at the Autobot base, the kids and Ratchet could only watch and listen.

'Optimus is down and MECH's going to grab the Dingus!' exclaimed Miko.

'OK . . .' Jack exhaled. 'Come on. Think,' he said to himself, turning away. 'All right, if MECH wants the Dingus – they have to get on the train.'

'What if we get onboard first?' suggested Miko with enthusiasm. 'You know – run some "human on human" interference!' She punctuated her speech with energetic air punches and looked at the others for their response.

Ratchet had heard enough. It was time to put his foot down. 'Absolutely *not*,' he said firmly.

'Yeah! That would be suicide . . .' Jack added, raising his eyebrows and shaking his head at the thought of it.

'*Hello?* The United States of *Meltdown*? *Lives* are at stake!' Miko replied forcefully, looking at the others as if they were not quite getting the point.

'Yes – *yours!*' exclaimed Ratchet. 'You expect me to 'Bridge you into a confined space travelling at ninety miles an hour?' The red and silver Autobot began to get quite worked up at the idea. 'I can't even *count* the number of ways that could go wrong . . . mass displacement trauma, twisted limbs, metal burn . . .'

The three humans stared at him. *Metal burn?* What was he talking about?

'Well, maybe not the last one . . .' Ratchet said a little sheepishly, realizing his mistake. 'Regardless, it is nearly impossible to fix GroundBridge coordinates on something moving at that speed.' He shook his head. He was not going to budge on this.

Raf was sitting at his laptop now, his fingers flying over the keyboard. 'Would it help if we had access to the train's coordinates?' he asked, intent on his work.

Just then, the blinking light that indicated a moving train popped back up on the track on the main display screen and with all the essential information streamed down the side of it.

'Well . . .' Ratchet paused. He had not seen that coming, and it definitely would make the job a whole lot easier . . .

As the freight train rushed along the tracks, an armed soldier patrolled the cargo car that the Dingus was travelling in. Not much was going on in there and there was nothing to report. Little did he know that trouble was on its way . . .

As Silas's chopper caught up with the moving train, he turned to one of his men. 'Immobilize them!' he ordered, and the masked man who had been standing at the open doorway raised his weapon and fired out one of the discs that they had used on Optimus' trailer.

The metal disc shot through the air and

then implanted its spikes into the side of one of the cargo cars. The disc lit up as it was activated and sent out a number of purple energy rays that travelled down the length of the freight train, crackling ferociously as they went.

The energy beams moved swiftly through the floor of the compartment that housed the Dingus and shot into the soldier's legs, sending electric pulses through his entire body. He dropped his gun immediately, his knees buckled beneath him, and he fell like a lead weight to the floor – out cold.

At that precise moment, at the other

end of the cargo car, a bright green
swirling light filled the carriage. It was
the GroundBridge portal. A split second
later, Miko and Jack were hurled out of it,

hitting the floor hard as they landed. They
struggled to their feet, shaking off the daze
from the ride, and the portal vanished
behind them. With no time to lose, Jack
whipped out his mobile phone.

'We're in,' he informed Raf.

'I read you, Jack,' came his friend's voice.

Just then came the sound of a chopper
at close range. Distracted, Jack lowered
the phone from his ear. He and Miko

exchanged worried glances and then slid the train door open to take a look.

As they suspected, the MECH chopper was approaching and it appeared to be preparing to land on the roof of the train.

'Raf – MECH's landing on *top* of the train!' Jack spoke urgently into his mobile phone.

In response, Raf typed furiously away at his laptop and glanced up at the train coordinates on the large display screen, thinking fast. 'In about twenty seconds you'll come to a fork. Brace yourselves!' he warned his friends.

Then he got back to his keyboard, concentrating hard on hacking into the train's computer data in an attempt to adjust its coordinates at just the right moment.

Meanwhile MECH, who had been following the train's coordinates on their own computer, were attempting the delicate process of landing the chopper on the train roof. The track was now running through a narrow ravine and the aircraft did not have that much space to manoeuvre. Plus, the landing struts were wider than the freight train, so it was a difficult operation even with the vehicle running in a straight line . . .

The pilot was about to touch down when Raf typed in a command on his laptop, and the train unexpectedly veered off down the left track, causing the chopper to overshoot and spin round, narrowly missing the ravine wall.

As the pilot righted the chopper, Silas peered angrily out of the window at the retreating train. 'What happened?' he demanded.

'Hacker,' the pilot explained. Then he hit a button on his control panel and grinned. '*Former* hacker.'

At that moment, back at HQ, a picture of a bomb and crossbones appeared both on Raf's laptop and the main control screen. He stared at it in amazement.

'What?' Raf asked in surprise as the screens starting flashing and an alarm sounded.

Then an electric charge shot out of his laptop keypad, causing him to hastily remove his hands, and the computer fizzed and died.

'And what have I been saying all along about Earth technology?' Ratchet said dismissively through the rising smoke, rolling his eyes at the boy.

The MECH chopper caught up with the freight train, and this time, without any interference, made a successful landing.

Miko and Jack had been watching its descent through the open door and then, when they heard the *thunk* on the metal roof, turned round quickly to see a laser begin to cut a hole through the ceiling of the car.

Jack sighed helplessly. 'So what did that buy us? *Ten seconds?*'

Miko shook her head. 'Raf is losing his touch,' she sighed.

Chapter Eight

RACE TO THE FINISH

Three of the Decepticon troopers were hanging onto Bulkhead's massive frame and he was crouched on the ground beneath them, protecting his head. Suddenly, with a great roar, he stood up and threw out his huge arms, scattering the Cons in three directions.

Meanwhile, another two of the troopers were running towards Arcee. Extending her gun arm, she fired out sonic blasts, wiping one of them out. One down, one Con to go.

Bumblebee was engaged in a fist fight with the sixth Decepticon, exchanging fierce blows that were sending sparks flying. He landed a particularly impressive right-hook on the enemy trooper which sent him hurtling to the edge of the cliff, but not quite over it.

About fifty metres below, Optimus was still lying face down on the ledge. At that moment, he stirred – shaking off the daze from his fall. He lifted his head a little, just enough to see down into the ravine below. He saw the track running through the middle of it, and in the distance there was the freight train, still racing along – with the MECH chopper on its roof!

Optimus raised himself up as quickly as he could – the Dingus was about to fall into the wrong hands, if MECH had not taken possession of it already, which meant that every second counted.

Miko and Jack stood and watched as the laser started to cut out the fourth side of the square in the cargo car ceiling. What could they do?

Looking around, Miko spotted an axe and a fire extinguisher on the wall behind them. She grabbed the axe with both hands and stood in a defensive pose – ready to fight off the intruders.

Following her lead, but a little less sure of himself than the feisty Japanese girl, Jack lifted the heavy fire extinguisher off the wall and struck a similar pose. As the metal square fell to the ground and the blue sky above the train was revealed, Jack's stomach began to do nervous back-flips. How could two teenagers hope to defeat trained assailants?

At that moment, three masked MECH men appeared, and glared down at them through the hole in the ceiling.

'Do you want a slice of this?' Miko growled at them, swinging the axe as she spoke. 'Well, do you?'

Jack cautiously waved the fire extinguisher at them, trying to act as tough as his friend. 'Yeah, what she said!' he spluttered.

The MECH men stared down at them in disbelief, vaguely amused by what they saw.

Just then, the pilot, who had landed the chopper one car back, spotted an enormous red and blue robot running down the side of the ravine parallel to the train.

'Sir!' he said urgently, alerting his leader.

Silas watched as Prime switched into Big Rig mode to achieve maximum speed, and then he issued a direct order.

'Retreat,' he said – commanding all his men to fall back. He knew that if he chose to, the powerful robot could pick up both the chopper and the men and crush them easily. They had no choice but to remove themselves from the scene.

Miko and Jack could not believe their eyes as the three MECHs retreated from the roof of the cargo train, and moments later they saw the chopper take off. The two friends leaned out of the train to take a better look at the disappearing aircraft. Neither of them were aware that Optimus was pursuing the train.

'Whoa!' Miko said in amazement,

looping her arm through Jack's. 'We were pretty fierce!'

Meanwhile, Silas had armed himself with one of MECH's futuristic weapons. 'First rule of combat,' he said grimly, lifting it to his shoulder. 'Never leave the enemy with the spoils.'

As far as he was concerned, if they could not have the Dingus, then nobody else would have it either. With that, he leaned out of the chopper and fired a missile at the train track ahead. The warhead met its target and smashed into the track, sending rocks flying and the rail twisting away from the ground.

The teenagers heard the *boom* of the explosion and saw the plume of smoke that immediately rose from the destroyed track.

'Whoa!' Jack pulled out his mobile and spoke urgently into it: 'Ratchet – MECH blew the train track! You need to 'Bridge us out of here – the soldiers too.'

'We've lost contact with the train data . . .'

Ratchet explained, while Raf gazed hopelessly at his destroyed laptop. 'I can't 'Bridge you back without your coordinates,' the Autobot went on, sounding worried.

Jack just stared at the phone in his hand, not believing what he was hearing. Miko hung onto his arm; all the fight had gone out of her and she looked petrified.

'Optimus!' Ratchet spoke to his leader over the comms link. 'Jack and Miko are on that train and MECH has just blown the tracks.'

'I'm on my way,' Prime assured his fellow Bot. 'MAXIMUM OVERDRIVE!' he bellowed and dust trails blew up behind the truck as he accelerated away.

The teenagers were hanging out of their cargo car, assessing their options.

'Maybe we should jump?' suggested Miko.

'At ninety miles per hour?' replied Jack, his voice wavering.

'It's that or the impact of the meltdown – take your pick,' the Japanese girl responded, stating the facts.

Jack sighed and slumped back against the doorway. 'What were we *thinking* when we volunteered for this?' he said helplessly.

'Next time *you* need to do a better job of talking us out of these situations,' Miko said spikily.

Just then, the teenagers were alerted to the sound of a fast-approaching vehicle and stuck their heads out of the doorway to see Optimus racing past!

Chapter Nine

a new kind of decepticon

As Bulkhead dispatched the final Decepticon trooper by landing a blow that smashed him into the ground, Arcee and Bumblebee strode up behind him.

'Where's Optimus?' asked Arcee.

'He had a train to catch,' Agent Fowler informed them from his viewing point up on the ledge.

As he finally caught up with the head car of the freight train, Optimus changed into robot mode and thundered forwards, wrapping his massive arms around the front of the speeding vehicle. He angled one enormous foot onto the track in a bid to use it as a brake, and put all his strength into pulling the train to a standstill.

However, the train was just as large a mechanical beast as he was, and its momentum dragged him along with considerable speed.

Seeing the broken, twisted metal of the track ahead, Optimus renewed his efforts, groaning from the strain. There was an awful screeching sound as Prime dug his foot down harder on the metal track, and rocks tumbled away on either side.

Finally, with just millimetres to spare, the train ground to a dramatic halt, its nose poking over the end of the track. Optimus, who had collapsed down on his knees as the freight train stopped, immediately rose to his feet and strode back to check on his two human friends.

Miko and Jack looked up at him – overwhelmed with gratitude but a little embarrassed at their failed attempt to stop MECH. Satisfied they were safe, Optimus looked round when he heard the sound of approaching propeller wings.

He stared up at the MECH chopper and frowned.

'Well played, visitor,' Silas congratulated him, even though the Autobot could not hear his words. 'But MECH has the home advantage, and we will find a way to level the playing field . . .' he said menacingly as a scan of Optimus appeared on his monitor screen and the computer starting producing diagrams of the robot. 'Even if we have to

open you up to see what makes
you tick . . .'

Optimus Prime watched the chopper
retreating, not taking his eyes off it until it
had disappeared into a speck in the distance.
He was experienced enough in war to
know that although they may have
defeated MECH this time, the battle was
far from over.

'Optimus – are you and the children
intact?' his friend's voice came over the
comm-link.

The Autobot leader nodded and glanced
down at Jack and Miko, who were also
gazing off into the distance, wanting to
make sure that the chopper really had
gone. The relieved teenagers started to
punch each other playfully and exchange
victorious high-fives.

'Intact, Ratchet,' Optimus said gently.
'Crisis averted. But the world in which
we live is a different one than previously
imagined.' His voice had taken on a

warning note. 'One which has formed its own Decepticons . . .' He paused, looking at the crater between the two sections of broken track. 'In human skin,' he finished – knowing that it would not be long before the Autobots would have to take on MECH again, and who knew what powerful weapons they would bring with them the next time . . .

Don't miss any of the action with these awesome new Transformers Prime titles!